The Uncanny Guest

By

E. T. A. Hoffmann

British Library Cataloguing-in-Publication Data
A catalogue record for this book is available from the
British Library

E. T. A. Hoffman

Ernst Theodor Wilhelm Hoffmann was born in Königsberg, East Prussia in 1776. His family were all jurists, and during his youth he was initially encouraged to pursue a career in law. However, in his late teens Hoffman became increasingly interested in literature and philosophy, and spent much of his time reading German classicists and attending lectures by, amongst others, Immanuel Kant.

In was in his twenties, upon moving with his uncle to Berlin, that Hoffman first began to promote himself as a composer, writing an operetta called Die Maske and entering a number of playwriting competitions. Hoffman struggled to establish himself anywhere for a while, flitting between a number of cities and dodging the attentions of Napoleon's occupying troops. In 1808, while living in Bamberg, he began his job as a theatre manager and a music critic, and Hoffman's break came a year later, with the publication of Ritter Gluck. The story centred on a man who meets, or thinks he has met, a long-dead composer, and played into the 'doppelgänger' theme – at that time very popular in literature. It was shortly after this that Hoffman began to use the pseudonym E. T. A. Hoffmann, declaring the 'A' to stand for 'Amadeus', as a tribute to the great composer, Mozart.

Over the next decade, while moving between Dresden, Leipzig and Berlin, Hoffman produced a great range of both literary and musical works. Probably Hoffman's most well-known story, produced in 1816, is 'The Nutcracker and the Mouse King', due to the fact that – some seventy-six years later - it inspired Tchaikovsky's ballet The Nutcracker.

In the same vein, his story 'The Sandman' provided both the inspiration for Léo Delibes's ballet Coppélia, and the basis for a highly influential essay by Sigmund Freud, called 'The Uncanny'. (Indeed, Freud referred to Hoffman as the "unrivalled master of the uncanny in literature.")

Alcohol abuse and syphilis eventually took a great toll on Hoffman though, and – having spent the last year of his life paralysed – he died in Berlin in 1822, aged just 46. His legacy is a powerful one, however: He is seen as a pioneer of both Romanticism and fantasy literature, and his novella, Mademoiselle de Scudéri: A Tale from the Times of Louis XIV is often cited as the first ever detective story.

The Uncanny Guest

A storm was raging through the heavens, announcing the coming of winter, whirling black clouds on its wings, which dashed down hissing, rattling squall-showers of rain and hail.

"Nobody will come to-night," said Madame von G. to her daughter Angelica, as the clock struck seven. "They would never venture out in such weather. If your father were but home!"

Almost as she was speaking, in came Captain Moritz von E. (a cavalry officer), followed by a young Barrister, whose brilliant and inexhaustible fund of humour and wit was the life and soul of the circle which was accustomed to assemble every Thursday evening in Colonel von G.'s house. So that, as Angelica said, there was little cause to be sorry that the less intimate members of the circle were away, seeing that the more welcome ones had come.

It felt very chilly in the drawing-room. The lady of the house had had a fire lighted, and the tea-table brought.

"I am sure," she said, "that you two gentlemen, who have been so courageous as to come to see us tonight through such a storm, can never be content with our wretched tea. Mademoiselle Marguerite shall make you a brew of that good, northern beverage which can keep any sort of weather out." Marguerite--a young French lady, who was "companion" to Angelica, for the sake of her language, and other lady-like accomplishments, but who was only about her own age, or

7

barely more--came, and performed the duty thus entrusted to her. So the punch steamed, while the fire sparkled and blazed; and the company sate down round the little tea-table.

A shiver suddenly passed through them--through each and all of them; and they felt chilled. Though they had been talking merrily before they sat down, there fell now upon them a momentary silence, during which the strange voices which the storm had called into life in the chimney whistled and howled with marvellous distinctness.

"There can be no doubt," said Dagobert (the young barrister), "that the four ingredients, Autumn, a stormy Wind, a good fire, and a jorum of punch, have, when taken together, a strange power of causing people to experience a curious sense of awesomeness."

"A very pleasant one, though," said Angelica. "At all events, I do not know a more delightful sensation than the sort of strange shiveriness which goes through one when one feels--heaven knows how, or why--as if one were suddenly casting a glance, with one's eyes open, into some strange, mystic dream-world."

"Exactly," said Dagobert; "that delicious shiveriness was exactly what came over all of us just now; and the glance into the dream-world, which we were involuntarily making at that moment, made us all silent. It is well for us that we have got it over, and that we have come back so quickly from the dream-world to this charming reality, which provides us with this grand liquid." He rose, and, bowing politely to Madame von G., emptied the glass before him.

"But," Moritz said, "if you felt all the deliciousness of that species of shudder, and of the dreamy condition accompanying it (as Miss Angelica and I did), why shouldn't you be glad to prolong it?"

"Let me say, my dear friend," Dagobert answered, "that the kind of dreaminess which we have to do with in this instance is not that in which the mind, or spirit, goes losing and sinking itself in all kinds of vague labyrinths of complexity of wondrous, calm enjoyment. The storm-wind, the blazing fire, and the punch are only the predisposing causes of the onsetting of that incomprehensible, mysterious condition--deeply grounded in our human organism--which our minds strive, in vain, to fight against, and which we ought to take great care not to allow ourselves to yield to over much. What I mean is, the fear of the supernatural. We all know that the uncanny race of ghosts, the haunters, choose the night (and particularly in stormy weather), to arise from their darksome dwellings, and set forth upon their mysterious wanderings. So that we are right in expecting some of those fearsome visitants just at a time like this."

"You do not mean what you say, of course," Madame von G. answered; "and I need not tell you that the sort of superstitious fear which we so often, in a childish way, feel, is not in any degree inherent in our organization as human beings. I am certain that it is chiefly traceable to the foolish stories of ghosts, and so forth, which servants tell us while we are children."

"No, Madame," Dagobert answered; "those tales--

9

which we enjoyed more than any others which we heard as children--would never have raised up such an enduring echo in us if the strings which re-echo them had not existed within us to begin with. There is no denying the existence of the mysterious spirit-world which lies all around us, and often gives us note of its Being in wondrous, mystic sounds, and even in marvellous sights. Most probably the shudder of awe with which we receive those intimations of that spirit-world, and the involuntary fear which they produce in us, are nothing but the result of our being hemmed in--imprisoned--by our human organization. The awe and the fear are merely the modes in which the spirit imprisoned within our bodies expresses its sorrow thereat."

"You are a spirit-seer, a believer in all those things--like all people who have lively imaginations," said Madame von G. "But if I were to go the length of admitting, and believing, that it is permitted that an unknown spirit-world should reveal its existence to us by means of sounds and sights, I should still have to say that I am unable to comprehend why that mysterious realm, and its denizens, should stand in such a relation to us that they bring merely paralyzing fear and horror upon us."

"Perhaps," Dagobert said, "it is the punishment inflicted on us by that mother from whose care and discipline we have run away. I mean, that in that golden age when our race was living in the most perfect union with all nature, no dread or terror disturbed us, for the simple reason that in the profound peace and perfect harmony of all created things, there was nothing hostile that could cause us any such emotion. I was mentioning strange spirit-sounds; but why is it that all the real nature-tones--of whose origin and causes we can give the most complete account--sound to us like the most piercing sorrow, and fill our hearts with the profoundest dread? The most remarkable of those nature-tones is the air-music, or, as it is called, the 'devil-voice,' heard in Ceylon and the neighbouring countries, spoken of by Schubert in his 'Glances at the Night-side of Natural Science.' This nature-tone is heard on calm and bright nights, sounding like the wail of some human creature lamenting in the deepest distress. It seems to come sometimes from the most remote distance, and then again to be quite close at hand. It affects the human intelligence so powerfully that the most self-controlled cannot help feeling the deepest terror when they hear it."

"Yes," said Moritz, "it is so. I have never been in Ceylon, certainly, or in any of the neighbouring countries; but I have heard that terrible nature-sound; and not only I, but every one else who heard it, felt just that precise effect which Dagobert alludes to."

"I should be extremely obliged to you," said Dagobert, "and you would probably convince Madame von G. also, if you would not mind telling us what happened."

"You know," Moritz said, "that I served the campaign in Spain under Wellington, with a mixed force of English and Spanish cavalry against the French. The night before the battle of Vittoria I was bivouacking in the open country.

Being wearied to death by the long march we had made during the day, I had fallen into a deep sleep of exhaustion, when I was awakened by a piercing cry of distress. I naturally thought--and it was the only idea that came into my mind- -that what I heard was the death-cry of some wounded soldier near me; but the comrades who were lying round me were all snoring, and there was no other sound to be heard. The first gleams of the dawn were breaking through the deep darkness, and I got up and strode away over the bodies of the sleepers, thinking that I might perhaps come across the wounded man, whoever he was, who had uttered that cry. It was a singularly calm night, and only most gradually and imperceptibly did the morning breeze begin to move, and to cause the leaves to tremble. Then a second cry, like the former--a long wail of woe--came ringing through the air, and died away in the remotest distance. It was as though the spirits of the slain were rising up from the battlefield, and wailing their boundless sorrow out into the wide heaven. My breast throbbed, was overwhelmed by an inexpressible awe; all the sorrow which I had ever heard exhaled from all human breasts was nothing in comparison with that heart-piercing wail. Our comrades now awoke from their sleep, and, for the third time, that terrible cry of sorrow arose, and filled the whole air, more fearful and awful than before. We were all smitten with the profoundest fear; even the horses were terrified; they snorted and stamped. Many of the Spaniards fell on their knees and prayed aloud. One of the English officers told us that he had several times met with this phenomenon in southern countries; and that it was of electrical origin, and there would probably be a change in the weather. The Spaniards, with their bent towards the supernatural, heard in it the mighty voices of supernatural beings, announcing great events about to happen. In this they were confirmed when, next day, the battle came thundering in upon them, with all its horrors."

"Is there any occasion." Dagobert said, "to go to Ceylon, or to Spain, to hear these marvellous Nature-tones of sorrow and complaining? Surely the howling of the storm-wind, the rattling of the hail, the groanings and creakings of the vanes are just as capable of filling us with profound terror as are those other Nature-tones we have been speaking of. Listen to that weird music which some hundreds of fearful voices are organing down this chimney; or to the strange little spirit-like ditty which the tea-urn is just beginning to sing."

"Oh! most ingenious indeed!" cried Madame von G. "Even into the very tea-urn Dagobert conjures spirits which render themselves cognisable to us by fearful cries of woe."

"But he is not far wrong, dear mother!" Angelica said. "I could very soon be seriously frightened at the extraordinary way in which that whistling, and rattling, and hissing is going on in the chimney; and the little tune which the tea-urn is singing, in such a tone of profound sorrow, is--to me--so eery and uncomfortable, that I shall go and blow out the spirit lamp, that there may be an end of it at once."

Angelica rose: her handkerchief fell. Moritz quickly picked it up and handed it to her. She allowed a glance, full of soul, from her heavenly eyes to rest upon him; he took her hand, and pressed it fervently to his lips.

At that moment Marguerite shuddered convulsively, as if touched by some electric current, and allowed the glass of punch, which she had just poured out for Dagobert, to drop from her hand. It shattered to atoms on the floor. She cast herself down at Madame von G.'s feet sobbing bitterly--said she was a stupid creature, and implored that she might be allowed to go to her room. She said that what they had been talking about had made her frightened and nervous--although she had not understood it; that she felt frightened still--as if she could not stay in the room--though she could not explain why; that she was feeling unwell, and would like to get to bed. So saying, she kissed Madame von G.'s hands, and bedewed them with the tears she was shedding.

Dagobert felt the painfulness of the incident, and the necessity of giving matters a different turn. He, too, fell at Madame von G.'s feet, and in the most pathetic voice at his command, begged forgiveness for the culprit. As regarded the stain of punch on the floor, he vowed that he would put waxed brushes on his feet in the morning, and go figuring athwart the boards in the most exquisite tours, and steps that ever inspired the brain of a court dancing-master.

Madame von G., who had at first been looking very grave over Marguerite's mishap, strange as it seemed, and inexplicable, cleared up a little at Dagobert's words. She gave each of them her hand with a smile and said, "Rise, and wipe away your tears. You are forgiven, Marguerite; you have this champion of yours to thank that I do not inflict a very severe punishment upon you. But I can't let you go altogether scot free. If you are a little out of sorts, you must try to forget it. I shall ordain you to stay here, be more assiduous than before at filling the gentlemen's glasses with the punch, and, above all things, you must reward your champion and defender with a kiss, in token of your sincere gratitude."

"So that Virtue is its own reward," Dagobert said, with a comic pathos, as he took Marguerite's hand. "All I ask of you, beauteous lady," he continued, "is to believe that the world contains (though you might be sceptical on the subject) legal luminaries of such a heroic sort that they do not hesitate a moment to offer themselves up a sacrifice at the shrine of Innocence and Truth. But we must obey the commands of our fair judge, from whose award there is no appeal." And he impressed a fugitive kiss upon Marguerite's lips, and then led her back to her seat with much solemnity. Marguerite, blushing like a rose, laughed very heartily; but the bright tears still stood in her eyes.

"Stupid fool that I am," she cried in French, "have I not got to do whatever Madame von G. bids me? I will keep perfectly calm. I will go on making their punch. I will listen to their ghost-stories without being in the least afraid."

"Bravo, angelic child," cried Dagobert. "My heroism has infected you, and the sweetness of your lips has inspired me. My imagination has unfolded new wings, and I feel ready to serve up the most awful events and mysteries from the 'Regno di Pianto.'"

"I thought we had done with this unpleasant subject," said Madame von G.

"Oh no, mother dear," cried Angelica eagerly; "please to let Dagobert go on! I am exactly like a child about those things. I don't know anything I so delight in as a nice ghost story--something that makes all one's flesh creep."

"Oh, how I do like that!" Dagobert cried. "Nothing is so utterly delightful in young ladies as their being tremendously superstitious, and easily frightened; and I should never dream of marrying a woman who was not terribly afraid of ghosts."

"You were saying a little while ago, dear Dagobert," said Moritz, "that we ought to guard ourselves against--or take care how we allow ourselves to get into--that dreamy state of awe which is the commencement of spirit-fear--the dread of the superhuman, the ghostly world. You have still got to explain to us the why."

"If there is, at the commencement of it, any real cause for that sense of awesomeness--which is at first so thoroughly blended up with the dreamily pleasurable--it by no means remains at that stage. Soon there supervenes a deadly fear--a horror which makes the hair stand on end; so that the said pleasurable feeling at the commencement would seem to be the fascination of temptation with which the Spirit World lures us on and ensnares us. We were talking of certain Nature-tones which are capable of explanation, and of their fearsome effect upon our senses. But we at times hear sounds more extraordinary, of which the origin and cause are indiscoverable by us, and which produce in us the profoundest awe and terror. All reassuring ideas--such as that they proceed from some animal in pain, or are produced by currents of air, or other natural causes--are useless and of no avail. Every one, I presume, has experienced that, in the night, the very faintest sound, if only it occurs at regular intervals with pauses between, completely drives away sleep, and goes on increasingly stirring up one's inward disquiet till it reaches the point of complete disorganization of the faculties. Not very long ago I had to spend a night, on a journey, at an inn, where the landlord put me in a nice, comfortable, lofty, airy bedroom. In the middle of the night I started up from my sleep, wide awake. The moon was shining brightly in at the window, which was uncurtained, so that I could see every article of the furniture, and even the minutest objects in the room. There was a sound as of water dropping into some metallic dish. I lay and listened. The drops went on falling at regular, measured intervals, drip, drip, drip. My dog, who was lying under the bed, crept out, and went about the room whimpering and crying, scratching on the walls and on the floor. I felt as if streams of icy water were running all through me, and the cold perspiration dripped from my brow. However, I collected myself by a great effort, and--after first of all giving a good loud shout--I got out of bed, and went forward to the middle of the room. There the drops seemed to be falling close in front of me, or rather I should say right through me into the metal, of which I heard the reverberation ringing loud and clear as they fell. Then, overcome by terror, I crept back, somehow, to the bed, and covered myself up with

17

the bedclothes. And then it seemed to me that the dropping-
-still going on at the same regular intervals--grew gradually
fainter and fainter, and died away as if in the distance. I fell
into a deep sleep, out of which I did not wake till it was
bright daylight in the morning. The dog had come and lain
down close beside me in bed, and did not move till I got up,
when he jumped up too, barking vigorously, as if he had got
over his terror of the previous night. It occurred to me that
it might only be to me that the (doubtless) natural cause
or causes of this strange sound were a mystery, and I told
the landlord of my adventure--of which I still felt the terror
in all my frame. I ended by saying that he could, no doubt,
explain the whole affair to me, but that he ought to have told
me of it beforehand. He turned as pale as a sheet, and begged
me never to tell any one what had happened to me, as he
would risk the loss of his customers. He said many travellers
had complained about that sound, which they had heard on
bright moonlight nights--that he had examined everything
with the utmost care and attention, and even had the floor of
that room and the adjoining one taken up, as well as making
inquisition into everything in the neighbourhood, without
coming upon the faintest trace of anything to account for
this awe-inspiring noise. It had not been heard for nearly a
year before the night I speak of, and he had been flattering
himself that the Principle--whatever it might be--which was
haunting the room had ceased its operation. But seeing, to
his great alarm, that in this he was mistaken, he determined
that he would never, in any circumstances, allow anybody to

pass the night there again."

"Oh! how terrible!" cried Angelica, shuddering like one in the cold stage of an ague. "That is really most terrible! Oh! I am sure I should have died if anything like that had happened to me! But I have often woke up from sleep, suddenly, feeling an indescribable, inexplicable alarm and anxiety, as if I had been going through something terrible and alarming; and yet, I had not the slightest idea what it was that I had been going through, nor the very faintest recollection of any fearful dream, or anything of that kind. Rather I seemed to be waking from some condition of complete unconsciousness, like death."

"I know that feeling perfectly well," Dagobert said. "Perhaps it points straight to the effect upon us of psychical influences external to us, to which we are compelled to yield ourselves up, whether we choose or not. Just as the mesmeric subject has no remembrance of the mesmeric sleep, or of anything which happens in it. Perhaps that sense of fear and anxiety which we feel on awaking (as we have said), of which the cause is hidden from us, may be the lingering echo of some mighty spell which has forced us out of ourselves."

"I remember very distinctly," Angelica said, "some four years ago, the night before my fourteenth birthday, awaking in a condition of that kind. I could not shake off the terror of it for several days afterwards. But I strove in vain to remember anything about my dream (if dream it was, that had so terrified me). I knew, and I know quite well, that in the very dream itself I had told several people--my own dear mother amongst them--what the dream was, several times. But all I could remember when I woke was that I had told the dream. I could not recall the slightest trace of what the dream had been."

"This strange psychical phenomenon," Dagobert said, "is closely connected with the magnetic principle."

"Our conversation is getting more and more dreadful," said Madame von G. "We are getting deep, and losing ourselves in matters I can't bear even to think about. Moritz, I must beg you to tell us something entertaining--outrageous even--that we may get away from this terrible region of the supernatural."

"I should be very happy to try," said Moritz, "if you will just allow me to tell one gruesome tale, which has been hovering on my lips for a long time. At this moment all my being is so filled with it that I feel that I could not talk about anything else."

"Discharge yourself, then," said Madame von G., "from the load of awesomeness which so weighs upon you. My husband will be home immediately, and then I should be so delighted to work through some battle or other with you and him, or to hear you talk in your absorbed manner about horses, or anything, to get me out of this overstrained condition into which all this supernatural stuff, I must admit, puts me."

"In my last campaign," said Moritz, "I made the acquaintance of a Russian Lieutenant-Colonel, a Livonian by birth, scarcely thirty, who, as chance willed it that we should be serving together before the enemy for a considerable time, soon became my very intimate friend. Bogislav--that was his Christian name--possessed every quality fitted to gain for him, everywhere, the highest consideration and the most sincere regard. He was tall and fine-looking, with an intellectual face. He possessed masculine beauty, much mental cultivation, and was kindliness itself, while brave as a lion. He could be particularly cheerful and entertaining, especially over a glass of wine; but there would often come over him, and overwhelm him, the thought of something terrible which had happened to him, leaving traces of the most intense horror and terror on his face. When this happened he would lapse into silence, leave the company, and stroll about up and down, alone. In the field, he used to ride all round the outposts at night, from one to another, restlessly, only yielding to sleep when completely exhausted; and as, in addition to this, he would often expose himself to the extremest danger, without any special necessity, and seemed to seek, in battle, death, which fled from him --for in the toughest hand-to-hand engagement never a bullet touched him; no sword-cut came near him--it seemed evident that his life had been marred by some irreparable bereavement, or perhaps some rash deed.

"We stormed, and captured, a fortified castle on the French territory, and remained quartered there for a day or two, to give the men some rest. The rooms where Bogislav was quartered were but a few steps from mine. In the night I was awakened by a gentle knocking at my door. I asked who

21

was there. My name was called out: I recognised Bogislav's voice, and went to let him in. There he stood in his night-dress, with a branched candlestick in his hand, pale as death, with his face distorted, trembling in every limb, unable to utter a word.

"'For heaven's sake! what has happened?--what is the matter, dearest Bogislav?' I cried. I took him to the arm-chair; made him swallow a glass or two of the full-bodied wine which was on the table; held his hand fast in mine, and spoke what comforting words I could, in my ignorance of the cause of his strange condition.

"He recovered himself by degrees, heaved a deep sigh, and then began, in a hollow voice: 'No! no! I shall go mad, unless death takes me; God knows I throw myself with eager longing into his arms. To you, my faithful Moritz, I will confide my fearful secret. I told you once that I was in Naples a good many years ago. There I met the daughter of one of the most distinguished families, and fell deeply in love with her. She returned my affection, and, as her parents gave their approval, I saw the fulfilment of my brightest hopes at hand. The wedding-day was fixed, when there appeared on the scene a Sicilian Count, who came between us with a most eager suit to my beloved and betrothed. I took him to task; he insulted me; we met, and I sent my sword through his body. I hastened to my love; I found her bathed in tears. She called me the accursed murderer of the man she had adored, and repelled me with every mark of disgust; screamed and wept in inconsolable sorrow; fell down fainting, as if stung by a scorpion, when I touched her hand. Who can describe my amazement! Her parents could not give the slightest explanation of the sudden change in her. She had never given any favourable heed to the Count's attentions.

"'Her father concealed me in his palazzo, and, with the most noble zeal, took care that I should be enabled to leave Naples undiscovered. Driven by all the furies, I pushed on to St. Petersburg without a halt. It is not the faithlessness of my love which plays havoc with my life. No! it is a terrible mystery. Since that unhappy day in Naples I have been dogged and pursued by the terrors of hell itself. Often by day, but still oftener by night, I hear--sometimes as if a long distance away, sometimes as if quite close beside me--a deep death-groan. It is the voice of the Count whom I killed! It makes my inmost soul quiver with horror. I hear that horrible sound distinctly, close to my ear, in the thick of the thunder of the heavy siege-guns, and the rattle of musketry, and all the wild despair of madness awakes within me. This very night----' Bogislav paused; and I, as well as he, was seized with the wildest horror; for there came to our hearing a long-sustained, heart-breaking wail of sorrow, as if proceeding from the stair outside. Then it was as if some one raised himself, groaning and sighing, with difficulty from the ground, and was coming towards us with heavy, uncertain steps.

"At this Bogislav started up from his seat, and, with a wild glow in his eyes, cried out, in a voice of thunder: 'Appear to me, abominable one, if you only will! I am more than a match for you, and all the spirits of hell that are at your disposal!'

"On this there came a tremendous crash, and----"

Just then the door of the drawing-room flew open with a startling noise.

And just as Ottmar read those words, the door of the summer-house in which the friends were sitting flew open, also with a startling noise, and they saw a dark form, wrapped in a mantle, approaching slowly, with noiseless footfalls, as of a spirit. They all gazed at this form, a little startled, holding their breaths.

"Is it right," said Lothair at length, when the full light of the lamps, falling upon his face, displayed their friend Cyprian. "Is it right to try to frighten good folks with foolish playing the ghost? However, I know, Cyprian, that you don't content yourself with studying spirits and all sorts of strange, visionary matters; you would often fain be a spook or ghost yourself. But where have you appeared from so suddenly? How did you find out that we were here?"

"I came back to-day from my journey," Cyprian said. "I went at once to see Theodore, Lothair, and Ottmar, but found none of them at home. In the fullness of my annoyance I ran out here into the open; and chance so willed it that, as I was returning to the town, I struck into the walk which leads past this summer-house. Then I seemed to hear a well-known voice; I peeped in at the window, and saw my worthy Serapion Brethren, and heard Ottmar reading 'The Uncanny Guest.'"

"What," interrupted Ottmar, "you know my tale?"

"You forget," said Cyprian, "that it was from me that you got the ingredients of the tale. It was I who told you of the 'Devil's Voice,' the aerial music of Ceylon, who even gave you the idea of the sudden appearing of the 'Uncanny Guest'; and I am curious to hear how you have worked out this 'Thema' of mine. You see that it was a matter of course that just when Ottmar had made the drawing-room door fly open I had necessarily to do the like, and appear to you myself."

"Not as an uncanny guest, though," said Theodore, "but as a true and faithful Serapion Brother, who, although he frightened me not a little, as I must perforce admit, is a thousand times welcome to me all the same."

"And," said Lothair, "if he insists on being a spirit, he must, at all events, not be an unquiet spirit, but sit down and drink tea, without making too much clattering with his cup, and listen to Ottmar, as to whose tale I am all the more curious, that this time it is a working up of a thema given to him by another."

Theodore, who was still easily excited after his recent illness, had been affected by Cyprian's proceedings rather more than was desirable. He was deadly pale, and it was evident that he had to put some constraint on himself to appear at his ease.

Cyprian saw this, and was not a little concerned at what he had done. "The truth is," he said, "that I had not thought about our friend's having only recently recovered, and hardly that, from a severe illness. I was acting contrarily to my own fundamental principle, which totally prohibits the perpetration of jokes of this description, because it has often happened that the terrible serious reality of the spirit-world has come gripping in into jokes of this kind, resulting in very terrific things. I remember, for instance----"

"Stop! stop!" cried Lothair. "I can't have any more interruptions. Cyprian is on the point of carrying us away, after his manner, into that dark world of spells where he is at home. Please to go on with your story, Ottmar." Ottmar went on reading.

And in came a man, dressed in black from top to toe, with a pallid face, and a set, serious expression. He went up to Madame von G. with the most courtly bearing of a man of the highest rank, and in well-selected terms, begged her to pardon him for having been so long in arriving, though his invitation was of such old standing--but that, to his regret, he had been detained by having to pay an unavoidable visit first. Madame von G., unable to recover all in a moment from the start which his entry had caused her, murmured a few indistinguishable words, which seemed to amount to saying, would the stranger be kind enough to take a seat. He drew a chair close to her, and opposite to Angelica, sat down, and let his eyes pass over every member of the company. Every one felt paralysed; none could utter a word. Then the stranger began to speak, saying that he felt he stood doubly in need of excuses; firstly, for arriving at such a time, and, secondly, for having made his entrance in such a sudden manner, and so startlingly. The latter, however, he was not to blame for, inasmuch as the door had been thrown open in

26

that violent manner by the servant whom he had found in the hall. Madame von G., overcoming with difficulty the eery feeling with which she was seized, inquired whom she had the honour of welcoming. The stranger seemed not to notice this question, his attention being fixed on Marguerite, who had suddenly become changed in all her ways and bearing, kept tripping and dancing close up to the stranger, and telling him, with constant tittering and laughter, and with much volubility, in French, that they had all been in the very thick of the most delightful ghost-stories, and that Captain Moritz had just been saying that some evil spectre ought to make its appearance at the very instant when he had come in. Madame von G., feeling all the awkwardness of having to ask this stranger, who had said he came by invitation, as to his name and so forth, but more distressed and rendered uncomfortable by his presence, did not repeat her question, but reprimanded Marguerite for her behaviour, which almost passed the limits of the "convenable." The stranger put a stop to Marguerite's chatter, turning to the others, and leading the conversation to some event of indifference which had happened in the neighbourhood. Madame von G. answered him. Dagobert tried to join in the conversation, which soon dragged painfully along in detached, interrupted sentences; and during this, Marguerite kept trilling couplets of French chansons, and seemed to be trying steps, as if remembering the "tours" of the newest gavotte, while the others were scarcely capable of moving. They all felt their breasts oppressed; the presence of the stranger weighed upon them like the sultry oppressiveness which precedes a thunderstorm. The words died on their lips when they looked at the deathly pale face of this uncanny guest. The markedly foreign accent with which he spoke both French and German indicated that he was neither a German nor a Frenchman.

Madame von G. breathed freely, with an enormous sense of relief, when at length horses were heard drawing up at the door, and the voice of her husband, Colonel von G., was distinguishable.

When the Colonel came in, and saw the stranger, he went up to him quickly, saying, "Heartily welcome to my house, dear Count." Then turning to his wife, he said, "This is Count S., a very dear friend of mine; I made his acquaintance in the north, but met him afterwards in the south."

Madame von G., whose anxiety began to be relieved, assured the Count, with pleasant smiles, that it was only because her husband had omitted to tell her of his visit that he had been received perhaps a little strangely, and not as a welcome friend ought to have been. Then she told the Colonel how the conversation had been running all the evening upon the supernatural; how Moritz had been telling a dreadful story of events which had happened to him and a friend of his, and that, at the very moment when he had been saying, "There came a tremendous crash," the door had flown open, and the Count had come in.

"Very good indeed," said the Colonel, laughing; "they thought you were a ghost, dear Count! I fancy I see traces of alarm and nervousness about Angelica's face still, and Moritz looks as though he had scarcely shaken off the excitement of the story he was telling. Even Dagobert does not seem quite in his ordinary spirits. Really, Count, it is a little too bad to take you for a revenant; don't you think so?"

"Perhaps," the Count replied; "I really may have something more or less ghostly about me. A good deal is being said nowadays, about people who, by virtue of some peculiar psychical quality, possess the power of influencing others, so that they experience very remarkable effects. I may be endowed with such a power."

"You are not serious, my dear Count," said Madame von G. "But there is no doubt that people are discovering very wonderful mysteries nowadays."

"People are pampering their curiosity, and weakening their minds over nursery tales and absurd fancies," was the Count's reply. "We ought all to take care not to allow ourselves to be infected by this curious epidemic. However, I interrupted this gentleman at the most interesting point of his story, and as none of his hearers would like to lose the finale, the explanation of the mystery, I would beg him to go on with it."

To Captain Moritz this stranger Count was not only uncomfortable and uncanny, but utterly repugnant, in all the depths of his being. In his words he found--all the more that he gave them out with a most irritating, self-satisfied smile--something indescribably contemptuous and insulting; and he replied, in an irritated tone, and with flashing eyes, that he feared his nursery tales might interfere with the pleasantness-

-the sense of enjoyment--which the Count had introduced into the circle, so that he would prefer to say no more.

The Count seemed scarcely to notice what Moritz said. Playing with the gold snuff-box which he had taken in his hand, he asked Madame von G---- if the "lively" young lady was French. He meant Marguerite, who kept dancing about the room, trilling. The Colonel went up to her and asked her, half aloud, if she had gone out of her senses. Marguerite slunk, abashed, to the tea-table, and sat down there quite quiet. The Count now took up the conversation, and spoke, in an entertaining manner, of this and the other events which had recently happened. Dagobert was scarcely able to put in a word. Moritz stood, red as fire, with gleaming eyes, as if waiting eagerly for the signal of attack. Angelica appeared to be completely immersed in the piece of feminine "work" at which she had set herself to labour. She did not raise an eyelid. The company separated in complete discomfort.

"You are a fortunate man," Dagobert cried, when he and Moritz were alone together. "Doubt no longer that Angelica is much attached to you. Clearly did I read in her eyes to-day that she is devotedly in love with you. But the devil is always busy, and sows his poisonous tares amongst the blooming wheat. Marguerite is on fire with an insane passion. She loves you with all the wild, passionate pain which only a fiery temperament is capable of feeling. The senseless way in which she behaved tonight was the effect of an irresistible outbreak of the wildest jealousy. When Angelica let fall the handkerchief--when you took it up and gave it to her--when you kissed her hand--the furies of hell possessed that poor Marguerite. And you are to blame for that. You used formerly to take the greatest pains to pay every kind of attention to that very beautiful French girl. I know well enough that it was only Angelica whom you had in your mind. Still, those falsely directed lightnings struck, and set on fire. And now the misfortune is there; and I do not know how the matter will end without terrible tumult and trouble."

"Marguerite be hanged (if I may use such an expression)," said Moritz. "If Angelica loves me--and ah! I can't believe, quite, that she does--I am the happiest and the most blest of men, and care nothing about all the Marguerites in the world, nor their foolishnesses neither. But another fear has come into my mind. This uncanny, stranger Count, who came in amongst us like some dark, gloomy mystery-- doesn't he seem to place himself, somehow, most hostilely between her and me? I feel, I scarce know how, as if some reminiscence came forward out of the dark background--I could almost describe it as a dream--which reminiscence, or dream, whichever it may be, brings this Count to my memory under terrible circumstances of some sort. I feel as though, wherever he makes his appearance, some awful misfortune must come flashing out of the depths of the darkness as a result of his conjurations. Did you notice how often his eyes rested on Angelica, and how, when they did, a feeble flush tinted his pallid cheeks, and disappeared again rapidly? The monster has designs upon my darling; and that is why the words which he addressed to me sounded so insulting. But I will oppose him and resist him to the very death!"

Dagobert said the Count was a supernatural sort of fellow, no doubt, with something very eery and spectral about him, and that it would be as well to keep a sharp look-out on his proceedings, though, perhaps, he thought there was less in, or behind, him than one would suppose; and that the uncanny feelings which everybody had experienced with regard to him were chiefly attributable to the excited state in which they had all been when he made his appearance. "Let us face all this disquieting affair," said Dagobert, "with firm courage and unshakable confidence. No dark power will bend the head which holds itself up with true bravery and indomitable resolution."

A considerable time had elapsed. The Count, whose visits to the Colonel's house increased in frequency, had rendered himself almost indispensable. It was universally agreed, now, that the accusation against him of being uncanny recoiled on those who made it. "He might very well have styled us uncanny people, with our white faces and odd behaviour," as said Madame von G----. Everything he said evinced a store of the most valuable and various information; and although, being an Italian, he spoke with a foreign accent, his command of the German language was most perfect and fluent. His narratives had a fire which bore the hearers irresistibly along, so that even Moritz and Dagobert, hostile as were their feelings to this stranger, forgot their repugnance to him when he talked, and when a pleasant smile broke out over his pale, but handsome and expressive face, and they hung upon his lips, like Angelica and the others.

The Colonel's friendship with him had arisen in a way which proved him to be one of the noblest-minded of men. Chance had brought them together in the far north, and there the Count, in the most unselfish and disinterested manner, came to the Colonel's aid in a difficulty in which he found himself involved, which might have had the most disastrous consequences to his fortune, if not to his good name and honour. Deeply sensible of all that he owed him, the Colonel hung on him with all his soul.

"It is time," the Colonel said to his wife one day when they were alone together, "that I should tell you the principal reason why the Count is here. You remember that he and I, when we were in P----, four years ago, grew more and more intimate and inseparable, so that at last we occupied two rooms which opened one into the other. He happened to come into my room one morning early, and he saw the little miniature of Angelica, which I had with me, lying on my writing-table. As he looked more and more closely at it, he lost his self-command in a strange way. Not able to answer me, he kept gazing at it. He could not take his eyes from it. He cried out excitedly that he had never seen a more beautiful creature--had never before known what love was--it was now blazing up in the depths of his heart. I jested about the extraordinary effect of the picture on him--called him a second Kalaf, and congratulated him on the fact that my good Angelica was not a Turandot. At last I told him pretty clearly that at his time of life--for, though not exactly elderly, he could not be said to be a very young man--this romantic way of falling in love with a portrait rather astonished me. But he vowed most vehemently--nay, with every mark of that passionate excitement, almost verging on insanity, which belongs to his country--that he loved Angelica inexpressibly, and, if he were not to be dashed into the profoundest depths of despair, I must allow him to gain her affection and her hand. It is for this that the Count has come here to our house. He fancies he is certain that she is not ill-disposed to him, and he yesterday laid his formal proposal before me. What do you think of the affair?"

Madame von G---- could not explain why his latter words shot through her being like some sudden shock. "Good heavens," she cried, "that Count for our Angelica! that utter stranger!"

"Stranger!" echoed the Colonel with darkened brow; "the Count a stranger! the man to whom I owe my honour, my freedom, nay, perhaps my life! I know he is not quite so young as he has been, and perhaps is not altogether suited to Angelica in point of age; but he is of high lineage, and rich, very rich."

"And without asking Angelica," said Madame von G----. "Very likely she may not have any such liking for him as he, in his fondness, imagines."

The Colonel started from his chair, and placed himself in front of her with gleaming eyes. "Have I ever given you cause to imagine," he said, "that I am one of those idiotic, tyrannical fathers who force their daughters to marry against their inclinations, in a disgraceful way? Spare me your absurd romanticisms and sentimentalities. Marriages may be made without any such extraordinary, fanciful love at first sight, and so forth. Angelica is all ears when he talks; she looks at him with most kindly favour; she blushes like a rose when he kisses her hand, which she willingly leaves in his. And that is how an innocent girl expresses that inclination which truly blesses a man. There is no occasion for any of that romantic love which so often runs in your sex's heads in such a disturbing fashion."

"I have an idea," said Madame von G----, "that Angelica's heart is not so free as, perhaps, she herself imagines it is."

"Nonsense," cried the Colonel, and was on the point of breaking out in a passion, when the door opened, and Angelica came in, with the loveliest smile of the most ingenuous simplicity. The Colonel, at once losing all his irritation, went to her, took her hand, kissed her on the brow, and sat down close beside her. He spoke of the Count, praising his noble exterior, intellectual superiority, character, and disposition; and then asked her if she thought she could care for him. She answered that at first he had appeared very strange and eery to her, but that now those feelings had quite disappeared, and that she liked him very much.

"Heaven be thanked then!" cried the Colonel. "Thus it was ordained to turn out, for my comfort, for my happiness. Count S--- loves you, my darling child, with all his heart. He asks for your hand, and you won't refuse him." But scarcely had he uttered those words when Angelica, with a deep sigh, sank back as if insensible. Her mother caught her in her arms, casting a significant glance at the Colonel, who gazed speechless at the poor child, who was as pale as death. But she recovered herself; a burst of tears ran down her cheeks, and she cried, in a heart-breaking voice, "The Count! the terrible Count! oh, no, no; never, never!"

As gently as possible the Colonel asked her why it was that the Count was so terrible to her. Then Angelica told him that at the instant when he had said that the Count loved her, that dream which she dreamt four years before, on the night before her fourteenth birthday--from which she awoke in such deadly terror without being able to remember the images or incidents of it in the very slightest--had come back to her memory quite clearly.

"I thought," she said, "I was walking in a beautiful garden where there were strange bushes and flowers which I had never seen the like of before. Suddenly I found myself close before a wonderful tree with dark leaves, large flowers, and a curious perfume something like that of the elder. Its branches were swaying and making a delicious rustling, and it seemed to be making signs inviting me to rest under its shade. Irresistibly impelled by some invisible power, I sank down on the grass which was under the tree. Then strange tones of complaint or lamenting seemed to come through the air, stirring the tree like the touch of some breeze; and it began to utter sighs and moans. And I was seized by an indescribable pain and sorrow; a deep compassion arose in my heart, I could not tell why. Then, suddenly, a burning beam of light darted into my breast, and seemed to break my heart in two. I tried to cry out, but the cry could not make its way from my heart, oppressed with a nameless anguish--it became a faint sigh. But the beam which had pierced my heart was the gleam of a pair of eyes which were gazing on me from under the shade of the branches. Just then the eyes were quite close to me; and a snow-white hand became visible, describing circles all round me. And those circles kept getting narrower and narrower, winding round me like threads of fire, so that, at last, the web of them was so dense and so close that I could not move. At the same time I felt that the frightful gaze of those terrible eyes was assuming the mastery over my inmost being, and utterly possessing my whole existence and personality. The one idea to which it now clung, as if to a feeble thread, was, to me, a martyrdom of death-anguish. But the tree bent down its blossoms towards me, and out of them spoke the beautiful voice of a youth, which said, 'Angelica! I will save you--I will save you--but----'"

Angelica was interrupted. Captain von P---- was announced. He came to see the Colonel on some matter of duty. As soon as Angelica heard his name she cried out with the bitterest sorrow, in such a voice as bursts only from a breast wounded with the deepest love-anguish--while tears fell down her cheeks--"Moritz! oh, Moritz!"

Captain von P---- heard those words as he came in; he saw Angelica, bathed in tears, stretch out her hands to him. Like a man beside himself he dashed his forage cap to the ground, fell at Angelica's feet, caught her in his arms, as she sank down overwhelmed with rapture and sorrow, and pressed her fervently to his heart.

The Colonel contemplated this little scene in speechless amazement. Madame von G---- said: "I thought this was how it was; but I was not sure!"

"Captain von P----," said the Colonel angrily, "what is there between you and my daughter?"

Moritz, quickly recovering himself, placed Angelica--more dead than alive--gently down on the couch, picked up his cap, advanced to the Colonel with a face red as fire, and eyes fixed on the ground, and declared that he loved Angelica unutterably; but that, upon his honour, until that moment, not a word approaching to a declaration of his feelings had crossed his lips. He had been but too seriously doubtful as to its being possible that Angelica could return his love. He said it was only at this moment--which he could not possibly have anticipated--that the bliss accorded to him by heaven had been fully disclosed to him; and that he trusted he should not be repulsed by the noblest hearted of mankind, the tenderest of fathers, when he implored him to bestow his blessing on a union sealed by the purest and sincerest affection.

The Colonel gazed at Moritz, and then at Angelica, with looks of gloom; then he paced up and down with folded arms like one who strives to arrive at a resolution. He paused before his wife, who had taken Angelica in her arms and was whispering to her words of consolation.

"What," he inquired, "has this silly dream of yours to do

with Count----?"

Angelica threw herself at his feet, kissed his hands, bathed them in her tears, and said, half-audibly, "Oh, father! dearest father! those terrible eyes which mastered my whole being were the Count's eyes. It was his spectral hand which wove round me those meshes of fire. But the voice of comfort which spoke to me out of the perfumed blossoms of the wondrous tree, was the voice of Moritz--my Moritz!"

"Your Moritz!" cried the Colonel, turning so quickly that he nearly threw Angelica down. He continued, speaking to himself in a lower tone: "Thus a father's wise resolve, and the offer of a grand and noble gentleman, are to be cast to the winds, for the sake of childish imaginations, and a clandestine love affair." And he walked up and down as before. At last, addressing Moritz, he said--

"Captain von P----, you know very well what a high opinion of you I have. I could not have wished for a better son-in-law. But I have promised my daughter to Count S----, to whom I am bound by the deepest obligations by which one man can be bound to another. At the same time, please do not suppose that I am going to play the part of the obstinate and tyrannical father. I shall hasten to the Count at once. I shall tell him everything. Your love will be the cause of a cruel difference between me and this gentleman. It may cost me my life. No matter; it can't be helped. Wait here till I come back."

Moritz warmly declared that he would sooner face death a hundred times than that the Colonel should run the very slightest risk; but the Colonel hurried away without reply.

As soon as he had gone, the lovers fell into each other's arms, and vowed unalterable fidelity. Angelica said that it was not until her father told her of the Count's views with regard to her, that she felt, in the depths of her soul, how unspeakably precious and dear Moritz was to her, and that she would rather die than marry any one else. Also that she had felt certain for a long time, that he loved her just as deeply. Then they both bethought themselves of all the occasions when they had given any betrayal of their love for each other; and, in short, were in a condition of the highest enjoyment and blissfulness, like two children, forgetting all about the Colonel and his anger and opposition. Madame von G—— -, who had long watched the growth of this affection, and approved of Angelica's choice with all her heart, promised, with deep emotion, to leave no stone unturned to prevent the Colonel from entering into an alliance which she abhorred, without precisely knowing why.

When an hour or so had passed, the door opened and, to the surprise of all, Count S—— came in, followed by the Colonel, whose eyes were gleaming. The Count went up to Angelica, took her hand, and looked at her with a smile of bitter pain. Angelica shrank, and murmured almost inaudibly, "Oh! those eyes!"

"You turn pale, Mademoiselle," said the Count, "just as you did when first I came into this house. Do you truly look upon me as a terrible spectre? No, no; do not be afraid of me, Angelica. I do but love you with all the fervour and passion of a younger man. I had no knowledge that you had given away your heart, when I was foolish enough to make an offer for your hand. Even your father's promise does not give me the slightest claim to a happiness which it is yours alone to bestow. You are free, Mademoiselle. Even the sight of me shall no longer remind you of the moments of sadness which I have caused you. Soon, perhaps to-morrow, I shall go back to my own country."

"Moritz! My Moritz!" Angelica cried in the utmost joy and delight, and threw herself on her lover's breast. The Count trembled in every limb; his eyes gleamed with an unwonted fire, his lips twitched convulsively; he uttered a low inarticulate sound. But turning quickly to Madame von G---- with some indifferent question, he succeeded in mastering his emotion.

But the Colonel cried, again and again, "What nobility of mind! What loftiness of character! Who is there like this man of men--my heart's own friend for ever!" Then he pressed Moritz, Angelica, and his own wife, to his heart, and said laughingly, that he did not care to hear another syllable about the wicked plot they had been laying against him, and hoped, too, that Angelica would have no more trouble with spectral eyes.

It being now well on in the day, the Colonel begged Moritz and the Count to remain and have dinner. Dagobert was sent for, and arrived in high spirits.

When they sat down to table, Marguerite was missing. It appeared she had shut herself up in her room, saying she was unwell and unable to join the company. "I do not know," said Madame von G----, "what has been the matter with Marguerite for some time; she has been full of the strangest fancies, laughing and crying without apparent reason. Really, she is at times almost unendurable."

"Your happiness is Marguerite's death," Dagobert whispered to Moritz.

"Spirit-seer!" answered Moritz in the same tone, "do not mar my joy."

The Colonel had never been in better spirits or happier, and Madame von G---- had never been so pleased in the depths of her heart, relieved as she was from anxieties which had often been present with her before. When, in addition to this, Dagobert was revelling in the most brilliant high-spirits, and the Count, forgetting his pain, suffered the stores of his much experienced mind to stream forth in rich abundance. It will be seen that our couple of lovers were encircled by a rich garland of gladness.

Evening was coming on, the noblest wines were pearling in the glasses, toasts to the health of the betrothed pair were drunk enthusiastically; when suddenly the door opened and Marguerite came tottering in, in white night-gear, with her hair down, pale, and distorted, like death itself.

"Marguerite, what extraordinary conduct!" the Colonel cried.

But, paying no heed to him, she dragged herself up to Moritz, placed her ice-cold hand on his breast, laid a gentle kiss on his brow, murmured in a faint, hollow voice, "The kiss of the dying brings luck to the happy bridegroom," and sank on the floor.

"This poor foolish girl is in love with Moritz," Dagobert whispered to the Count, who answered--

"I know. I suppose she has carried her foolishness so far as to take poison."

"Good heavens!" cried Dagobert, starting up and hurrying to the arm-chair where they had placed poor Marguerite. Angelica and her mother were busy besprinkling her and rubbing her forehead with essences. When Dagobert went up she opened her eyes.

"Keep yourself quiet, my dear child," said Madame von G----; "you are not very well, but you will soon be better-- you will soon be better!"

Marguerite answered in a feeble, hollow voice, "Yes; it will soon be over. I have taken poison."

Angelica and her mother screamed aloud.

"Thousand devils!" cried the Colonel. "The mad creature! Run for the doctor! Quick! The first and best that's to be found; bring him here instantly!"

The servants, Dagobert himself, were setting off in all haste.

"Stop!" cried the Count, who had been sitting very quietly hitherto, calmly and leisurely emptying a beaker of his favourite wine--the fiery Syracuse. "If Marguerite has taken poison, there is no need to send for a doctor, for, in this case, I am the very best doctor that could possibly be called in. Leave matters to me."

43

He went to Marguerite, who was lying profoundly insensible, only giving an occasional convulsive twitch. He bent over her, and was seen to take a small box out of his pocket, from which he took something between his fingers, and this he gently rubbed over Marguerite's neck and the region of her heart. Then coming away from her, he said to the others, "She has taken opium; but she can be saved by means which I can employ."

By the Count's directions Marguerite was taken upstairs to her room, where he remained with her alone. Meanwhile, Madame von G---- had found the phial which had contained the opium-drops prescribed some time previously for herself. The unfortunate girl had taken the whole of the contents of the phial.

"The Count is really a wonderful man," Dagobert said, with a slight touch of irony. "He divines everything. The moment he saw Marguerite he knew she had taken poison, and next he knew exactly the name and colour of it."

In half-an-hour the Count came and assured the company that Marguerite was out of danger, as far as her life was concerned. With a side-glance at Moritz, he added that he hoped to remove all cause of mischief from her mind as well. He desired that a maid should sit up with the patient, whilst he himself would spend the night in the next room, to be at hand in case anything fresh should transpire; but he wished to prepare and strengthen himself for this by a few more glasses of wine; for which end he sat down at table with the other gentlemen, whilst Angelica and her mother, being upset by what had happened, withdrew.

The Colonel was greatly annoyed at this silly trick, as he called it, of Marguerite's, and Moritz and Dagobert felt very eery and uncanny over the whole affair; but the more out of tune they were the more did the Count give the rein to a joviality which had never been seen in him before, and which, in sober truth, had a certain amount of gruesomeness about it.

"This Count," Dagobert said to Moritz, as they walked away, "has a something most eerily repugnant to me about him, in some strange inexplicable way. I cannot help a feeling that there must be something exceedingly mysterious connected with him."

"Ah!" said Moritz, "there is a weight as of lead on my heart. I am filled with a dim foreboding that some dark mischance threatens my love."

That night the Colonel was aroused from sleep by a courier from the Residenz. Next morning he came to his wife, looking rather pale, and constraining himself to a calmness which he was far from feeling, said, "We have to be parted again, dearest child. There's going to be another campaign, after this little bit of a rest. I shall have to march off with the regiment as soon as ever I can, perhaps this evening."

Madame von G---- was greatly startled; she broke out into bitter weeping. The Colonel said, by way of consolation, that he felt sure this campaign would end as gloriously as the last--that he felt in such admirable spirits about it that he was certain nothing could go amiss. "What you had better do," he said, "is, take Angelica with you to the country-house, and stay there till we send the enemy to the rightabout again. I am providing you with a companion who will keep you amused, and prevent your feeling lonely. Count S---- is going with you."

"What!" cried Madame von G----. "Good heavens! the Count to go with us!--Angelica's rejected lover--that deceitful Italian, who is hiding his annoyance in the bottom of his heart, only to bring it out in fullest force at the first proper opportunity; this Count who--I cannot say why-- seems more intensely antipathetic to me since yesterday than ever?"

"Good God!" the Colonel cried; "there really is no bearing with the nonsensical ideas--the silly dreams--which your sex gets into its head. The magnanimity of soul of a man of his firmness and fineness of character is too much for you to comprehend. The Count passed the whole night in the room next to Marguerite's, as he said he should do. He was the first person I told the news of the fresh campaign to. It would scarcely be possible for him to go home now. This was very annoying to him, and I gave him the option of going to our country-place and staying there. He accepted my offer, after much hesitation, and gave me his word of honour that he would do everything in his power to take care of you, and make the time of our separation pass as quickly as possible. You know what obligations I am under to him. My country-place is, just now, a real asylum for him; could I refuse him that?"

Madame von G---- could say nothing further. The Colonel did as he had said he would. In the course of the evening the trumpets sounded boot and saddle, and every description of nameless pain and heart-breaking sorrow came upon the loving ones.

A few days after, when Marguerite had recovered, the three ladies went off to the country-house. The Count followed, with a number of servants.

And at first, the Count, showing the utmost delicacy of feeling, was careful never to enter the ladies' presence except when they sent for him specially; at all other times he remained in his own rooms, or went for solitary walks.

At first the campaign seemed to go rather in favour of the enemy, but important successes were soon scored against him, and the Count was always the very first to hear the news of those operations, and particularly the most accurate and minute intelligence of what was happening to the regiment which the Colonel commanded. In the bloodiest engagements neither the Colonel nor Moritz had met with so much as a scratch; and the despatches from headquarters confirmed this.

Thus the Count always appeared to the ladies in the character of a heavenly messenger of victory and good-fortune; besides this, all his behaviour betokened the most deep and sincere attachment to Angelica, which he exhibited to her as the tenderest of fathers might have done, occupied constantly about her happiness. Both she and her mother were compelled to admit to themselves that the Colonel's opinion of this tried friend of his was the correct one, and that all their--and other people's--prejudices against him had been the most preposterous fancies. At the same time Marguerite seemed to be quite cured of her foolish passion, and to have become the same gay, talkative, sprightly French lady whom we saw at an earlier period.

A letter from the Colonel to his wife, enclosing one from Moritz to Angelica, dispelled the last remnant of anxiety. The enemy's capital city was captured, and an armistice established.

Angelica was floating in a sea of blissfulness; and always it was the Count who spoke of the brave deeds of Moritz, and of the happiness which was opening its blossoms for the lovely future bride. After such speeches he would take Angelica's hand, press it to his heart, and ask if he were still as hateful to her as ever. With blushes and tears she would assure him that she had never hated him, but that she had loved Moritz too deeply and exclusively not to dread the idea of any other suitor for her hand. And the Count would say, very solemnly and seriously, "Look on me as your true, sincere, fatherly friend, Angelica," breathing a gentle kiss upon her forehead, which she suffered without ill-will; for it felt much like one of her father's kisses, which he used to apply about the same place.

It was almost expected that the Colonel would very soon be home again, when a letter from him arrived containing the terrible news that Moritz had been set upon by some armed peasants, as he was passing with his orderly through a village. Those peasants shot him down at the side of the brave trooper, who managed to fight his way through; but the peasants carried Moritz away. Thus the joy with which the house was inspired was suddenly turned into the deepest and most inconsolable sorrow.

The Colonel's household was all in busy movement from roof to ceiling. Servants in gay liveries were hurrying to and fro; carriages filled with guests were rattling into the courtyard, the Colonel in person receiving them with his new order on his breast.

In her room upstairs sate Angelica in wedding-dress, beaming in the full pride of her loveliness: her mother was with her.

"My dearest child," said the latter, "you have of your own free will accepted Count S---- as your husband. Much as jour father desired this, he has never at all insisted on it since poor Moritz's death; indeed, it seems to me as though he had had much of the feeling which (I cannot hide from you) I have had myself; it is utterly incomprehensible to me how you can have forgotten poor Moritz so soon. However, the time has come; you are giving your hand to the Count. Examine your own heart. It is not yet too late. May the remembrance of him whom you have forgotten never fall across your heart like some black shadow."

"Never," cried Angelica, while the tears ran down her cheeks, "never can I forget Moritz. Never; oh! never can I love as I loved him! What I feel for the Count is something totally different. I cannot explain how it is that the Count has made me feel this irresistible attachment to him; but feel it I do, in every fibre of my being. It is not that I love him: I do not; I cannot love him in the way I loved Moritz; but I feel as if I could not, and cannot live apart from him--without him--independently of him. That it is only through him that I can think and feel. A spirit voice seems perpetually enjoining me to cleave to him as a wife; telling me that I must do so, and that unless I do there is no further, or other life possible for me here below. And I obey this voice, which I believe to be the mysterious prompting of Providence."

The maid here came in to say that Marguerite, who had been missing since the early part of the morning, had not made her appearance yet, but that the Gardener had just brought a little note which she had given him, with instructions to deliver it when he had finished his work and taken the last of the flowers to the Castle. It was as follows:--

"You will never see me more; a dark mystery drives me from your house. I implore you--you, who have been to me as a tender mother--not to have me followed, or brought back by force. My second attempt to kill myself will be more successful than the first. May Angelica enjoy to the full that bliss, the idea of which pierces my heart. Farewell for ever! Forget the unfortunate Marguerite."

"What is this?" cried Madame von G----; "the poor soul seems to have set her whole mind upon destroying our happiness. Must she always come in your way just as you are going to give your hand to the man of your choice? Let her go; the foolish, ungrateful thing, whom I treated and cared for as if she had been my own daughter. I shall certainly never trouble my head about her any more."

Angelica cried bitterly at the loss of her whom she had looked on as a sister; her mother implored her not to waste a thought on the foolish creature at such an important time.

The guests were assembled in the salon, ready, as soon as the appointed hour should come, to go to the little chapel where a catholic priest was to marry the couple. The Colonel led in the bride. Everyone marvelled at her beauty, which was enhanced by the simple richness of her dress. The Count had not arrived. One quarter of an hour succeeded another, and still he did not make his appearance. The Colonel went to the Count's rooms. There he found his valet, who said his master, just when he was fully dressed for the ceremony, had suddenly felt unwell, and had gone out for a turn in the park, hoping the fresh air would revive him, and forbidding him, the valet, to follow him.

The Colonel could not explain to himself why it was that this proceeding of the Count's fell on him with such a weight--why it was that an idea immediately came to him that something terrible had happened. He sent back to the house to say that the Count would come very shortly, and that a celebrated doctor, who was one of the guests, was to be privately told to come out to him as quickly as possible. As soon as he came, he, the Colonel and the valet, went to search for the Count in the park. Striking out of the main alley, they went to an open space surrounded by thick shrubberies, which the Colonel remembered to have been a favourite resort of the Count's; and there they saw him sitting on a mossy bank, dressed all in black, with his star sparkling on his breast, and his hands folded, leaning his back against an elder-tree in full blossom, staring, motionless, before him. They shuddered at the sight, for his hollow, darkly-gleaming eyes were evidently devoid of the faculty of vision.

"Count S----! what has happened?" the Colonel cried; but there was no answer, no movement, not the slightest appearance of respiration. The doctor hurried forward; tore off the Count's coat, waistcoat, and neckcloth, and rubbed his brow: turning then to the Colonel, he said in hollow tones, "Human help is useless here. He is dead!--there has been an attack of apoplexy!"

The valet broke out into loud lamentations. The Colonel, mastering his inward horror with all his soldierly self-control, ordered him to hold his peace, saying, "If we are not careful what we are about, we shall kill Angelica on the spot." He caused the body to be taken up and carried by unfrequented paths to a pavilion at some distance, of which he happened to have the key in his pocket. There he left it under the valet's charge, and, with the doctor, went back to the chateau again. Hovering between one resolve and another, he could not make up his mind whether to conceal the whole matter from Angelica, or tell her, calmly and quietly, the terrible truth.

When he came into the house he found everything in the utmost confusion and consternation. Angelica, in the middle of an animated conversation, had suddenly closed her eyes, and fallen into a state of profound insensibility. She was lying on a sofa in an adjoining room. Her face was not pale, nor in the least distorted; the roses of her cheeks bloomed brighter and fresher than ever, and her face shone with an indescribable expression of happiness and delight. She was as one penetrated with the highest blissfulness. The doctor, after observing her with the minutest carefulness of examination for a long while, declared that there was not the least cause for anxiety in her condition, nor the slightest danger. He said she was (although it was entirely inexplicable how she was) in a magnetized condition, and that he would not venture to awaken her from it: she would wake from it of her own accord presently.

Meanwhile mysterious whisperings arose amongst the guests. The sudden death of the Count seemed to have somehow got wind, and they all dispersed in gloomy silence. One could hear the carriages rolling away.

Madame von G----, bending over Angelica, watched her every respiration. She seemed to be whispering words, but none could hear or understand them. The doctor would not allow her to be undressed; even her gloves were not to be taken off; he said it would be hurtful even to touch her.

All at once she opened her eyes, started up from the sofa, and, with a resounding cry of "Here he is!" "Here he is!" went rushing out of the room, through the ante-chamber and down the stairs.

"She is out of her mind," cried Madame von G----. "Oh, God of Heaven, she is mad!" "No, no," the Doctor said, "this is not madness; there is something altogether unheard of taking place," with which he hastened after her down the steps.

He saw her speeding like an arrow, with her arms lifted up above her head, out of the gate and away along the broad high road, her rich lace-ornamented dress fluttering, and her hair, which had come down, streaming in the wind.

A man on horseback was coming tearing up towards her; when he reached her, he sprang from his horse and clasped her in his arms. Two other riders who were following him drew rein and dismounted.

The Colonel, who had followed the doctor in hot haste, stood gazing on the group in speechless astonishment, rubbing his forehead, as if striving to keep firm hold of his thoughts.

It was Moritz who was holding Angelica fast pressed to his heart; beside him stood Dagobert, and a fine-looking young man in the handsome uniform of a Russian General.

"No," cried Angelica over and over again, as the lovers embraced one another, "I was never untrue to you, my beloved Moritz." And Moritz cried, "Oh, I know that; I know that quite well, my darling angel-child. He enchanted you by his satanic arts."

And he more carried than led her back to the chateau, while the others followed in silence. Not till he came to the castle did the Colonel give a profound sigh, as if it was only then that he came fully to his senses; and, looking round him with questioning glances, said, "What miracles! what

54

extraordinary events!"

"Everything will be explained," said Moritz, presenting the stranger to the Colonel as General Bogislav von Se----n, a Russian officer, his most intimate friend.

As soon as they came into the chateau, Moritz, with a wild look, and unheeding the Colonel's alarmed amazement, cried out, "Where is Count von S----i?"

"Among the dead!" said the Colonel, in a hollow voice, "he was seized with apoplexy an hour ago."

Angelica shrank and shuddered. "Yes," she said, "that I know. At the very instant when he died I felt as though some crystal thing within my being shivered, and broke with a 'kling.' I fell into an extraordinary state. I think I must have gone on carrying that frightful dream (which I told you of) further, because, when I came to look at matters again, I found that those terrible eyes had no more power over me; the web of fire loosened and broke away. Heavenly blissfulness was all about me. I saw Moritz, my own Moritz; he was coming to me. I flew to meet him," and she clasped her arms round him as if she thought he was going to escape from her again.

"Praised be Heaven," said Madame von G----. "Now the weight has gone from my heart which was stifling it. I am freed from that inexpressible anxiety and alarm which came upon me at the instant when Angelica promised to marry that terrible Count. I always felt as though she were betrothing herself to mysterious, unholy powers with her betrothal ring."

General von Se----n expressed a desire to see the Count's

remains, and when the body was uncovered and he saw the pale countenance now fixed in death, he cried, "By Heaven, it is he! It is none other than himself."

Angelica had fallen into a gentle sleep in Moritz's arms, and had been carried to her bed, the doctor thinking that nothing more beneficial could have happened to her than this slumber, which would rest the life-spirits, overstrained as they had been. He considered that in this manner a threatening illness would be naturally dispelled.

"Now," said the Colonel, "it is time to solve all those riddles and explain all those miraculous events. Tell us, Moritz, what angel of Heaven has called you back to life?"

"You know," said Moritz, "all about the murderous and treacherous attack which was made upon me near S----, though the armistice had been proclaimed. I was struck by a bullet, and fell from my horse. How long I lay in that deathlike state I cannot tell. When I first awoke to a dim consciousness, I was being moved somewhere, travelling. It was dark night; several voices were whispering near me. They were speaking French. Thus I knew that I was badly wounded and in the hands of the enemy. This thought came upon me with all its horror, and I sank again into a deep fainting fit. After that came a condition which has only left me the recollection of a few hours of violent headache; but at last, one morning, I awoke to complete consciousness. I found myself in a comfortable, almost sumptuous bed, with silk curtains and great cords and tassels. The room was lofty, and had silken hangings and richly-gilt tables and chairs, in the old French style. A strange man was bending over me and looking closely into my face. He hurried to a bell-rope and pulled at it hard. Presently the doors opened, and two men came in, the elder of whom had on an old-fashioned embroidered coat, and the cross of Saint Louis. The younger came to me, felt my pulse, and said to the elder, in French, 'All danger is over; he is saved.' The elder gentleman now introduced himself to me as the Chevalier de T----. The house was his in which I found myself. He said he had chanced, on a journey, to be passing through the village at the very moment when the treacherous attack was made upon me, and the peasants were going to plunder me. He succeeded in rescuing me, had me put into a conveyance, and brought to his chateau, which was quite out of the way of the military routes of communication. Here his own body-surgeon had applied himself to the arduous task of curing me of my very serious wound in the head. He said, in conclusion, that he loved my nation, which had shown him kindness in the stormy revolutionary times, and was delighted to be able to be of service to me. Everything in his chateau which could conduce to my comfort or amusement was freely at my disposal, and he would not, on any pretence, allow me to leave him until all risk, whether from my wound or the insecurity of the routes, should be over. All that he regretted was the impossibility of communicating with my friends for the moment, so as to let them know where I was.

"The Chevalier was a widower, and his sons were not with him, so that there were no other occupants of the chateau but himself, the surgeon, and a great retinue of servants. It would only weary you were I to tell you at length how I grew better and better under the care of the exceedingly able surgeon, and how the Chevalier did everything he possibly could to make my hermit's life agreeable to me. His conversation was more intellectual, and his views less shallow, than is usually the case with his countrymen. He talked on arts and sciences, but avoided the more novel and recent developments of them as much as possible. I need not tell you that my sole thought was Angelica, that it burned my soul to know that she was plunged in sorrow for my death. I constantly urged the Chevalier to get letters conveyed to our headquarters. He always declined to do so, on account of the uncertainty of the attempt, as it seemed as good as certain that fighting was going on again; but he consoled me by promising that as soon as I was quite convalescent he would have me sent home safe and sound, happen what might. From what he said I was led to suppose that the campaign was going on again, and to the advantage of the allies, and that he was avoiding telling me so in words from a wish to spare my feelings. But I need only mention one or two little incidents to justify the strange conjectures which Dagobert has formed in his mind. I was nearly free from fever, when one night I suddenly fell into an incomprehensible condition of dreaminess, the recollection of which makes me shudder, though that recollection is of the dimmest and most shadowy kind. I saw Angelica, but her form seemed to be dissolving away indistinctly in a trembling radiance, and I strove in vain to hold it fast before me. Another being pressed in between us, laid herself on my breast, and grasped my heart within me, in the depths of my entity; and while I was perishing in the most glowing torment, I was at the same time penetrated with a strange miraculous sense of bliss. Next morning my eyes fell on a picture hanging near the bed, which I had never seen there before. I shuddered, for it was Marguerite beaming on me with her black brilliant eyes. I asked the servant whose picture it was, and where it came from. He said it was the Chevalier's niece, the Marquise de T----, and had always been where it was now, only I had not noticed it; it had been freshly dusted the day before. The Chevalier said the same. So that, whilst--waking or dreaming--my sole desire was to see Angelica, what was continually before me was Marguerite. It seemed to me that I was alienated, estranged, from myself. Some exterior foreign power seemed to have possession of me, ruling me, taking supreme command of me. I felt that I could not get away from Marguerite. Never shall I forget the torture of that condition.

"One morning, as I was lying in a window seat, refreshing my whole being by drinking in the perfume and the freshness which the morning breeze was wafting to me, I heard trumpets in the distance, and recognized a cheery march-tune of Russian cavalry. My heart throbbed with rapture and delight. It was as if friendly spirits were coming to me, wafted on the wings of the wind, speaking to me in lovely voices of comfort, as if a newly-won life was stretching out hands to me to lift me from the coffin in which some hostile power had nailed me up. One or two horsemen came up with lightning speed, right into the castle enclosure. I looked down, and saw Bogislav. In the excess of my joy I shouted out his name; the Chevalier came in, pale and annoyed, stammering out something about an unexpected billeting, and all sorts of trouble and annoyance. Without attending to him, I ran downstairs and threw myself into Bogislav's embrace.

"To my astonishment, I now learned that peace had been proclaimed a long time before, and that the greater part of the troops were on their homeward march. All this the Chevalier had concealed from me, keeping me on in the chateau as his prisoner. Neither Bogislav nor I knew anything in the shape of a motive for this conduct. But each of us dimly felt that there must be something in the nature of foul play about it. The Chevalier was quite a different man from that moment, sulky and peevish. Even to lack of good breeding, he wearied us with continual exhibitions of self-will, and naggling about trifles. Nay, when, in the purest gratitude, I spoke enthusiastically of his having saved my life, he smiled malignantly; and, in fact, his whole conduct was that of an incomprehensible eccentric.

"After a halt of eight-and-forty hours for rest, Bogislav marched off again, and I went with him. We were delighted when we turned our backs on the strange old-world place, which now looked to me like some gloomy, uncanny prison-house. But now, Dagobert, do you go on, for it is quite your turn to continue the account of the rest of the strange adventures which we have met with."

"How," began Dagobert, "can we doubt, and hesitate to believe in, the marvellous power of foreboding, and fore-knowing, events which lie so deep in man's nature? I never believed that my friend was dead. That Spirit or Intelligence (call it whatever you choose) which speaks to us, comprehensibly, from out our own selves, in our dreams, told me that Moritz was alive, and that, somehow and somewhere, he was being held fast in bonds of some most mysterious nature. Angelica's relations with the Count cut me to the heart; and when, some little time ago, I came here and found her in a peculiar condition, which, I am obliged to say, caused me an inward horror (because I seemed to see, as in a magic mirror, some terrible mysterious secret), there ripened in me a resolve that I would go on a pilgrimage, by land and water, until I should find my friend Moritz. I say not a word of my delight when I found him, on German ground, at A----, and in the company of General von S----en.

"All the furies of hell awoke in his breast when he heard of Angelica's betrothal to the Count; but all his execrations and heart-breaking lamentations at her unfaithfulness to him were silenced when I told him of certain ideas which I had formed, and assured him that it was in his power to set the whole matter straight in a moment. General von Se----en shuddered when I mentioned the Count's name to him, and when, at his desire, I described his face, figure, and appearance, he cried, 'Yes, there can be no further doubt. He is the very man!'"

"You will be surprised," here interrupted the General,

61

"to hear me say that this Count S----i, many years ago, in Naples, carried away from me, by means of diabolical arts, a lady whom I deeply and fondly loved. At the very instant when I ran my sword through his body, both she and I were seized upon by a hellish illusion which parted us for ever. I have long known that the wounds which I gave him were not dangerous in the slightest degree, that he became a suitor for the lady's hand, and, alas! that on the very day when she was to have been married to him, she fell down dead, stricken by what was said to be an attack of apoplexy."

"Good Heavens!" cried Madame von G----. "No doubt a similar fate was hanging over my darling child! But how is it that I feel this is so?"

"The voice of the boding Spirit tells you so, Madame," said Dagobert.

"And then," said Madame von G----, "that terrible apparition which Moritz was telling us of that evening when the Count came in in such a mysterious way?"

"As I was telling you then," said Moritz, "there fell a crashing blow. An ice-cold deathly air blew upon me, and it seemed to me that a pale indistinct form went hovering and rustling across the room, in wavering, scarcely distinguishable outlines. I mastered my terror with all the might of my reason. All I seemed to be conscious of was that Bogislav was lying stiff, cold, and rigid, like a man dead. When he had been brought back to consciousness, with great pains and trouble, by the doctor who was summoned, he feebly reached out his hand to me, and said, 'Soon, to-morrow at latest, all my sorrows will be over.' And it really happened as he said, though it was the will of Providence that it should come about in quite a different way to that which we anticipated. In the thick of the fighting, next morning, a spent ball struck him on the breast and knocked him out of his saddle. This kindly ball shattered the portrait of his false love, which he wore next to his heart, into a thousand splinters. His contusion soon healed, and since that moment Bogislav has been quite free from everything of an uncanny nature."

"It is as he says," said the General, "and the very memory of her who is lost to me does no more than produce in me that gentle sadness which is so soothing to the heart. But I hope our friend Dagobert will go on to tell you what happened to us further."

"We made all haste away from A----," Dagobert resumed, "and this morning, just as day was breaking, we reached the little town of P---, about six miles from this place, meaning to rest there for an hour or two, and then come on here. Imagine the feelings of Moritz and me when, from one of the rooms in the inn, we saw Marguerite come bursting out upon us, with insanity clearly written on her pallid face. She fell at Moritz's feet and embraced his knees, weeping bitterly, calling herself the blackest of criminals, worthy a thousand deaths. She implored him to end her life on the spot. Moritz repulsed her with the deepest abhorrence, and rushed away from the house."

"Yes," said Moritz, "when I saw Marguerite at my feet, all the torments of that terrible condition in which I had been at the Chevalier's came back upon me, goading me into a state of fury such as I had never known before. I could scarcely help running my sword through her heart; but I succeeded in mastering myself, and I made my escape after a mighty effort."

"I lifted Marguerite up from the floor," Dagobert continued, "and helped her to her room. I succeeded in calming her, and heard her tell me, in broken sentences, exactly what I had expected and anticipated. She gave me a letter from the Count, which had reached her the previous midnight. I have it here."

He produced it, and read it as follows:--

"Fly, Marguerite! All is lost! The detested one is coming quickly. All my science, knowledge, and skill are of no avail to me as against the dark fate and destiny about to overtake me at the very culminating point of my career.

"Marguerite, I have initiated you into mysteries which would have annihilated any ordinary woman had she endeavoured to comprehend them. But you, with your exceptional mental powers, and firm, strong will and resolution, have been a worthy pupil to the deeply experienced master. Your help has been most precious to me. It was through you that I controlled Angelica's mind, and all her inner being. And, to reward you, it was my desire to prepare for you the bliss of your life, according to the manner in which your heart conceived it; and I dared to enter within circles the most mysterious, the most perilous. I undertook operations which often terrified even myself. In vain. Fly, or your destruction is certain. Until the supreme moment comes I shall battle bravely on against the hostile powers. But I know well that that supreme moment brings to me instant death. But I will die all alone. When the supreme moment comes I shall go to that mysterious tree, under whose shadow I have so often spoken to you of the wondrous secrets which were known to me, and at my command.

"Marguerite, keep aloof from those secrets for evermore. Nature, terrible mother, angry when her precocious children prematurely pry into her secrets and pluck at the veil which covers her mysteries, throws to them some glittering toy which lures them on until its destroying power is directed against them. I myself once caused the death of a woman, who perished at the very moment when I thought I was going to take her to my heart with the most fervid affection; and this paralysed my powers. Yet, dolt that I was, I still thought I should find bliss here on earth. Farewell, Marguerite, farewell. Go back to your own country. Go to S----. The Chevalier de T---- will charge himself with your welfare and happiness. Farewell."

As Dagobert read this letter, all the auditors felt an inward shudder, and Madame von G---- said, "I shall be compelled to believe in things which my whole heart and soul refuse to credit. However, I certainly never could understand now it was that Angelica forgot Moritz so quickly and devoted herself to the Count. At the same time I cannot but remember that she was all the time in an extraordinary, unnatural condition of excitement, and that was a circumstance which

65

filled me with the most torturing anxiety. I remember that her inclination for the Count showed itself at first in a very strange way. She told me she used to have the most vivid and delightful dreams of him nearly every night."

"Exactly," said Dagobert. "Marguerite told me that, by the Count's directions, she used to sit whole nights by Angelica's bedside, breathing the Count's name into her ear very, very softly. And the Count would very often come into the room about midnight, fix a steadfast gaze on Angelica for several minutes together, and then go away again. But now that I have read you the Count's letter, is there any need of commentary? His aim was to operate psychically upon the Inner Principle by various mysterious processes and arts, and in this he succeeded, by virtue of special qualifications of his nature. There were most intimate relations between him and the Chevalier de T----, both of them being members of that secret society or 'school' which has a certain number of representatives in France and Italy, and is supposed to be descended from, or a continuation of, the celebrated P---- school. It was at the Count's instigation that the Chevalier kept Moritz so long shut up in his chateau, and practised all sorts of love-spells on him. I myself could go deeper into this subject, and say more about the mysterious means by which the Count could influence the Psychic Principle of others, as Marguerite divulged some of them to me. I could explain many matters by a science which is not altogether unknown to me, though I prefer not to call it by its name, for fear of being misunderstood. However, I had rather avoid all those subjects, to-day at all events."

"Oh, pray avoid them for ever," cried Madame von G----
. "No more reference to the dark, unknown realm, the abode
of fear and horror. I thank the Eternal Power, which has
rescued my beloved child, and freed us from the uncanny
guest who brought us such terrible trouble."

It was arranged that they should go back to town the
following day, except the Colonel and Dagobert, who stayed
behind to see to the burial of the Count's remains.

When Angelica had long been Moritz's happy wife, it
chanced that one stormy November evening the family, and
Dagobert, were sitting round the fire in the very room into
which Count S---- had made his entry in such a spectral
fashion. Just as then, mysterious voices were piping, awakened
by the storm-wind in the chimney.

"Do you remember?" said Madame von G----.

"Come, come," cried the Colonel; "no ghost stories, I
beg." But Angelica and Moritz spoke of what their feelings
had been on that evening long ago; of their having been
so devotedly in love with each other, and unable to help
attaching the most overweening importance to every little
incident which occurred: how the pure beam of that love of
theirs had been reflected by everything, and even the sweet
bond of alarm wove itself out of loving, longing hearts--and
how the Uncanny Guest, heralded by all the spectral voices
of ill-omen, had brought terror upon them. "Does it not
seem to you, dearest Moritz," said Angelica, "that the strange
tones of the storm-wind, as we hear them now, are speaking

to us, only of our love, in the kindliest possible tones?"

"Yes! yes!" said Dagobert, "and the singing of the kettle sounds to-night to me much more like a little cradle song than anything eerie."

Angelica hid her blushing face on Moritz's breast. And he--for his part--clasped his arm round his beautiful wife, and softly whispered, "Is there, here below, a higher bliss than this?"

"I see very plainly," said Ottmar, when he had finished, and the friends still sat in gloomy silence, "that my little story has not pleased you particularly, so we had better not say much more about it, but consign it to oblivion."

"The very best thing we could do," said Lothair.

"And yet," Cyprian said, "I must take up the cudgels for my friend. Of course you will say that I am to some extent mixed up in the matter--that Ottmar has taken a good many of the germs of the story from me, and on this occasion has been cooking in my kitchen, so that you won't be disposed to allow me to be a judge in the case. Yet, unless you mean to condemn everything without the slightest remorse, like so many Rhadamanthuses--you must admit, yourselves, that there is much in Ottmar's story which must be allowed to pass as genuinely Serapiontic; the beginning, for instance."

"Quite right," said Theodore; "the party round the tea-table may pass as from the life, as well as many other points during the course of the tale. But, to speak candidly, we have had a very large assortment of spectral characters such as the stranger Count, and it will soon be a difficult matter to go on giving them novelty and originality. He is too much like Alban in 'The Magnetizer.' You know the tale I mean, and indeed that story and Ottmar's have both the same motif. Wherefore I wish I might beg our Ottmar and you, Cyprian, to leave monsters of that sort out of the game in future. For Ottmar this will be possible, but for you, Cyprian, I am not so sure that it will. So that we shall have to allow you to serve us up a 'Spook' of the kind now and then, I suppose, only stipulating that it shall be truly Serapiontic, i.e. come out of the very inmost depths of your imagination. Moreover 'The Magnetizer' seems rhapsodical, but the 'Uncanny Guest' is rhapsodical in very truth."

"I must take up the cudgels for my friend in this respect too," said Cyprian, "and tell you that, in the very neighbourhood of this place where we are at this moment, there actually happened an event, not very long ago, by no means unlike the incidents of this story. Into a quiet happy group of friends, just when supernatural matters were forming the subject of conversation, there suddenly came a stranger, who struck every one as being uncanny and terrifying, notwithstanding his apparent everydayness, and seeming belonging to the common level. By his arrival this stranger not only spoiled the enjoyment of the evening in question, but subsequently destroyed the peace and happiness of the family for a long period. Even at this day deadly shudders seize a happy wife when she thinks of the crafty wickedness with which this person tried to entangle her in his nets. I told this at the time to Ottmar, and nothing made a greater impression on him than the moment when the stranger made his spectral entry, and the sense of the propinquity of the hostile Spiritual Principle seized upon every one present with a sudden terror. This moment came vividly to Ottmar's mind, and formed the groundwork of his tale."

"But," said Ottmar, "as a single incident is far from being a complete story--which ought to spring perfect and complete from its author's brain, like Minerva from the head of Jupiter--my tale is of course not worth much as a whole, and it is little to my credit, I suppose, that I took advantage of two or three incidents which really happened, weaving them--not without some little success perhaps--into a network of the imaginary."

"Yes," said Lothair, "you are right, my friend. A single striking incident is far from being a tale, just as one well-imagined theatrical situation is a long way from constituting a play. This reminds me of the way in which a certain playwright (who no longer walks this world, and whose terrible death certainly atoned for any shortcomings of his during his life, and reconciled his worst enemies to him) used to construct his pieces. In a company where I was present, he said, without any concealment, that he selected some one's good dramatic situation which occurred to him, and then, solely for the sake of that, hung a canvas round it and painted away upon it 'just whatever came in his head,' or 'as best he could,' to use his own expressions. This gave me a complete explanation of, and threw a dazzling flood of light upon, the whole character and inner being of that writer's pieces, particularly those of his later period. None of them is without some very happily devised central situation, but all round this the scenes, which he made up out of commonplace material, are woven like a loosely knitted web, although the hand of that weaver, skilled as it is in technique, is never to be mistaken."

"Never, say you?" remarked Theodore. "I have been always waiting and looking out for the points where that writer would abandon his commonplaces, and rise into the region of romance and true poetry. The most striking and melancholy instance of what I mean is the so-called Romantic Drama, 'Deodata'; a strange nondescript production, on which a clever composer ought not to have wasted capital music. There can be no more striking proof of the utter want of infelt poetry, of any conception of the higher dramatic life, than where the author of 'Deodata,' in his preface, finds fault with Opera because it is unnatural that people should sing on the stage, and next goes on to explain that he has been at pains to introduce the singing, which is incidental to it, always in a natural manner."

"De mortuis nil nisi bonum," said Cyprian, "let the dead repose in peace."

"And all the more," said Lothair, "that I see midnight is close at hand, and he might avail himself of that circumstance to give us a box or two on the ear (as he is said to have done to his critics in life) with his invisible fist."

Just then the carriage which Lothair had sent for on account of Theodore's still invalid condition, came rolling up, and the friends went back in it to town.